⊥ 3.8
P 2.0

Maxie, Rosie, and Earl—
PARTNERS IN GRIME

ALSO BY BARBARA PARK

My Mother Got Married (and Other Disasters)
Almost Starring Skinnybones
The Kid in the Red Jacket
Buddies
Beanpole
Operation: Dump the Chump
Skinnybones
Don't Make Me Smile

BARBARA PARK

Maxie, Rosie, and Earl —

Partners in Grime

Illustrations by Alexander Strogart

ALFRED A. KNOPF NEW YORK

Text copyright © 1990 by Barbara Park
Illustrations copyright © 1990 by Alexander Strogart
All rights reserved under International and Pan-American
Copyright Conventions. Published in the United States by
Alfred A. Knopf, Inc., New York, and simultaneously in
Canada by Random House of Canada Limited, Toronto.
Distributed by Random House, Inc., New York.

Book design by Mina Greenstein
Manufactured in the United States of America
10   9   8   7   6   5   4   3   2   1

Library of Congress Cataloging-in-Publication Data
Park, Barbara. Maxie, Rosie, and Earl—partners in
grime / by Barbara Park.   p.   cm.
Summary; When their disciplinary meetings with the
principal are postponed, three students skip school with
humorous results.
ISBN 0-679-80212-6 (trade)
ISBN 0-679-90212-0 (lib. bdg.)
[1. Behavior—Fiction.   2. Schools—Fiction.]   I. Title.
PZ7.P2197Max   1990   [Fic]—dc20   89-28027   CIP   AC

Contents

Maxie, Rosie, and Earl—
PARTNERS IN GRIME

Earl

Earl Wilber sat at his desk and doodled on the back of his reading workbook. The class was reading a social studies assignment out loud, but Earl wasn't sure what it was about. His doodle was taking all of his concentration. He was drawing a B-52 fighter plane dropping a bomb on the school.

Fifth grade wasn't fun. Not when you were a new kid. Not when you had no friends.

Earl had hated Dooley Elementary from the very beginning. On his first day of school, two girls ran by and called him Plumpy.

You big-fat stupids, thought Earl, making a fist. He didn't say it out loud, though. Earl was only brave in his head.

He didn't make friends easily. Not only was he shy, but new situations made him tense and sweaty. And whenever he was tense and sweaty, he almost always did something dumb. Like when it was his turn to stand at his desk and introduce himself, he clicked his heels like a soldier and saluted. He still didn't know why.

"You're trying too hard," his mother had told him when she drove him to school one morning. Then she handed him a Kleenex to wipe the perspiration from his top lip.

"Just be yourself, Earl. If you just relax and settle down, you'll have new friends in no time."

But of course Earl knew that wasn't true. Friends didn't flock around you just because you were all limp and relaxed. And anyway, being all limp and relaxed made Earl tense.

It's not like he hadn't tried to make friends. Last Tuesday at lunch, he had actually tapped Anthony Jabbort on the arm and offered him half of his cream-filled cupcake.

But Anthony had just wrinkled up his nose and said, "Gross! You've had your mouth all over it."

Things didn't get any better either. When he went back to class that afternoon, Mrs. Mota had asked Earl to read out loud in front of the entire class. Not exactly the kind of activity that made him relax.

They had been reading a story about a boy and his sailboat, when suddenly Earl heard his name called.

"Earl Wilber? Would you read the next paragraph for us, please?" Mrs. Mota asked.

Shocked, Earl looked up. What was she calling on him for? He hadn't even had his hand in the air!

His heart started pounding like crazy.

"Earl?" asked Mrs. Mota again.

Nervously, Earl studied his first sentence. *John sailed, himself.*

It didn't seem that hard. Simple, in fact. Maybe he could do it. Of course he could. Relax! Just relax!

Courageously, he wiped the sweat off his forehead and cleared his throat.

"*John soiled himself,*" he barked.

The whole class cracked up at once. Even

Mrs. Mota couldn't keep the corners of her mouth from turning up.

"Sailed!" he yelled quickly. "I mean, John *sailed*, himself!"

But it was too late. And the laughter was too loud. And Earl Wilber had wanted to die.

So that's why on this particular day—while the rest of the class was reading the social studies assignment—Earl Wilber was drawing a B-52 bomber blowing up the school. Because no matter what, he never wanted to read out loud again.

Don't think about it, he told himself, as his stomach churned nervously inside him. *Just keep your head down, and she won't notice you.* He drew a tank blowing up the water fountain on the playground.

"Earl Wilber?"

No. Oh no. It couldn't be!

Slowly, he raised his head.

Oh geez! Oh geez! Mrs. Mota was smiling right at him!

"Could you read for us, please, Earl?"

He couldn't believe it! Why did she keep doing this to him? What had he done to make her hate him so much?

He tried to swallow, but he couldn't. Little

beads of sweat popped out all over his forehead. The silence in the room was deadly. Earl's collar felt tight around his neck. He stretched it out so he could breathe.

"Page twenty-two, paragraph three," the teacher informed him.

Earl forced himself to look at his book. But the memory of what had happened the last time was still too fresh in his mind.

Mrs. Mota's eyes were on the clock. "We're waiting, Earl. I'd really appreciate it if you would just give it a try."

Suddenly, Earl shook his head no. He hadn't really planned on refusing. It just sort of happened.

Mrs. Mota raised her eyebrows.

"Earl?" she asked, not believing what she had just seen.

Earl gulped. Much to his horror, his head shook no again. It seemed to be on automatic pilot or something.

"No?" questioned the puzzled teacher. "Are you saying no, you won't read? No, you won't even try to read?"

Before he could reply, Mrs. Mota rose from her chair. As Earl watched her walk toward him, a little whimper escaped from his throat.

Back! he wanted to scream. Go back! I'll read, okay? But even though he opened his mouth, nothing came out.

A second or two later, Mrs. Mota was standing over him, glaring down at his doodle. She tapped her foot.

Panicking, Earl smoothed out the paper and offered it to her. "I made this for you," he sputtered desperately. But Mrs. Mota was already helping him out of his chair.

"I'm sorry, Earl, but I think you'd better come with me."

The next thing Earl knew, she had him by the hand and was leading him out the door. His palm was sweaty. He slipped from her grasp.

"I don't know what it was like at your last school," said Mrs. Mota, grabbing hold of Earl's wrist this time, "but at Dooley Elementary you don't say no when you're asked to read. At Dooley Elementary you at least give it a try. Maybe you'll understand our rules better if Mr. Shivers explains them to you personally."

That's when it hit him. He didn't know why it had taken him so long. But that was the first moment when Earl Wilber realized he was going to the principal's office!

Frantically, he tugged on his teacher's sweater. "No! I can't. I can't go there! My mother will kill me!"

But Mrs. Mota kept right on walking.

"I mean it, teacher," he said, temporarily forgetting her name. "You don't know her. She doesn't have a good sense of humor."

Mrs. Mota didn't seem to be listening.

"I'm sorry, okay?" he went on. "I changed my mind! I'll read now!"

They passed a poster hanging on the wall. Earl pointed. " 'Come to the Ice Cream Social!' " he read as they hurried by.

Mrs. Mota's expression softened a little. "I'm sorry, Earl. I really am," she replied. "I just think this is best."

With each new step toward the office, Earl's legs got weaker. He had to struggle to keep his knees from caving in beneath him.

He felt flushed and warm.

"I think I'm having a heart attack," he said breathlessly.

Mrs. Mota opened the door of the main office and swiftly led Earl to the secretary's desk.

The secretary, Mrs. Trumbull, eyed Earl as if he were a criminal. He fanned himself with his hand. "Could you call an ambulance, do you think?" he squeaked.

"Take a seat," she instructed him, pointing to a yellow plastic chair on the other side of the reception counter.

Earl whimpered again. Then he walked around the counter and sank down in the chair so the secretary couldn't see him.

Mrs. Mota looked at him a moment. Then she and Mrs. Trumbull started talking about him as if he weren't there.

"Mr. Shivers is really busy right now," the secretary told the teacher. "It may be a while before he's able to talk to the boy."

Mrs. Mota thought it over. "That's okay. It won't hurt Earl to sit here. He's got plenty to think about."

Mrs. Trumbull craned her neck to see over the counter. "Do you ride the bus, young man?"

Earl covered his face and shook his head no.

"Then there's no problem," she told Mrs. Mota. "If Mr. Shivers can't see him till after school, we'll just dismiss him from here."

Mrs. Mota nodded. Then she glanced at Earl one last time, and left the office.

Earl didn't wave good-bye.

The principal's door was closed. A small sign hung on the doorknob. It said: THE PRINCIPAL IS YOUR PAL. Earl squeezed his eyes shut.

Suddenly, the door opened and Mr. Shivers rushed into the room. He was tall and bald and wore a bright-green suit. Earl gulped. What sort of man would buy a suit like that? A weird man . . . a dangerous man. Earl trembled. An *insane* man.

Mr. Shivers whispered to his secretary a moment, then looked over at Earl and frowned.

He hurried back to his office door.

"Mr. Wilber, would you like to step in here, please?" he said, not sounding at all happy. "I'm a little short of time but I'll try to fit you in."

Earl couldn't talk. All the spit in his mouth had dried up, and his lips were stuck together.

Mr. Shivers stepped aside and let Earl pass. Once inside, he offered him a seat.

As Earl sat down, his top lip started to quiver. He tried to stop it, but he couldn't. It was a lip out of control.

"My secretary told me that Mrs. Mota brought you down here to talk to me," said the principal. "Is that correct?"

Earl quivered his lip at him.

Mr. Shivers folded his arms. "Why don't you tell me what happened?"

Earl covered his mouth to hide his lip. After a second, he opened his fingers slightly. "Is it warm in here to you?" he asked nervously.

Mr. Shivers cleared his throat. "Why are you here, Earl?" he asked more emphatically.

Earl could feel himself becoming almost rigid. He couldn't think at all. It was as if his brain had completely shut down.

"Why am I here? Why am I here?" he muttered, feeling confused and helpless without his brain.

That's when it happened. Something inside him snapped. He'd heard of people cracking up in times of stress, and now it was happening to him. Nothing was funny. Nothing at all. But for some reason Earl felt a horrible urge to laugh.

Stop it! Stop it! he ordered silently, panicking at the thought of breaking into giggles.
*This isn't funny! Now shut up and tell him
what happened, before it's too late!*

He took a deep breath.

"Um . . . well, let's see . . . uh . . . the
class was reading, and I didn't want to, so I
was . . . doodling."

Doodling. That did it. As soon as the word
was out of his mouth, Earl started to laugh.
Doodle. Suddenly it seemed like such a funny
word. Had it always been this funny? Doodle
. . . doodle . . . doodle . . .

Earl fought to regain control of himself, but
it was no use. And much to his horror, he
collapsed in a wild fit of hysteria.

It was the sloppy kind of laughter. The kind
with lots of nose snorts and pig snuffles. Desperately, he put both hands over his mouth,
but the noises exploded right through all ten
of his fingers, causing him to laugh even
louder. Completely out of control, Earl pulled
his shirt up over his face so the principal
couldn't see him.

Mr. Shivers drummed his fingers on his desk
and stared at Earl's stomach. He waited for

Earl to quiet down. It seemed like forever before the boy's hysterics finally began to taper
off.

"Hah, hah, hah, hah . . . hee, hee . . . hah
. . . heh, heh, heh . . . aaahhhhhh, hooooo."

Afraid to come out from beneath his shirt,
Earl blotted his eyes.

Mr. Shivers stood up. "Finished?"

Still hidden, Earl took a deep breath and
nodded his head.

"Good," said the principal, opening the office door. "Why don't you go back outside for
a few minutes, and we'll talk again after you're
completely settled down."

Earl dried his eyes one last time before
pulling his shirt back down where it be-
longed. Shakily, he stood. Then, looking only
at the floor, he hurried past the principal and
scrambled back into the yellow plastic chair
in the waiting room.

The secretary peered at him over her typewriter.

Feeling sick, Earl Wilber slumped down and
out of view.

Rosie

As Earl Wilber was sweating it out in the principal's office, Rosie Swanson sat in her classroom and took her weekly spelling test. After listening carefully to each word, she printed it neatly on her paper and then quickly spread her skinny arms across the top of her test so no one could see her answers. No one sat directly next to Rosie, but Judith Topper sat right in front of her. And with Judith Topper around, there was always a chance of cheating.

Judith was the worst speller in the room. She was always the first one to sit down during a spelling bee. Once, just to be nice, Mr. Jolly had asked her to spell the word *a*. Judith spelled it "e." On the way to her seat, she said she thought it had been a trick question.

In the front of the room, Mr. Jolly cleared his throat. "*Urgent*," he called, loud and clear. "The last spelling word is *urgent*."

Cautiously, Rosie pushed her red-framed glasses back up on the bridge of her nose. As she looked around, she ran her fingers through her wispy blond hair. Her bangs were too long, but she liked them that way. When your bangs were too long, you could stare at people through your hair and they never knew they were being watched.

When Rosie was sure that the coast was clear, she uncovered her test paper and printed URGENT in space number ten. She smiled. Another 100 percent, she thought proudly as she turned the paper facedown on her desk.

All of a sudden, Judith Topper began to squirm in her chair. A second later, she dropped her pencil on the floor and leaned down to pick it up. Once she was out of the teacher's view, she strained to see Lisa Graham's test paper in front of her.

Finally, she sat back up. Then Rosie watched as Judith erased her mistakes and copied the correct spellings.

Nothing made Rosie Swanson angrier than cheating. It just wasn't fair! Why should she spend her time studying for these stupid spelling tests, when cheaters like Judith ended up with the same grade?

Annoyed, Rosie cupped her hands around her mouth. "I sawwwww youuuu," she sang in Judith's ear.

Judith rolled her eyes. "Nerd," she said out of the corner of her mouth.

That did it! As soon as the coast was clear again, Rosie pulled out the little yellow note-pad she kept hidden in her desk and quickly wrote:

Dear Mr. J.
Judith T. cheated on her spelling test again.
                    Sincerely yours,
                    R. Swanson

Rosie folded the note into a little ball and used her thumb to press it into the palm of her hand. Then, grabbing a pencil out of her desk, she headed for the sharpener. As she passed Mr. Jolly's desk, she dropped the note into his center drawer.

Rosie smiled to herself. She was good at this. She really was.

The rest of the class was lining up for lunch. Rosie sharpened her pencil and rushed back to her desk to grab her lunch sack. She was just on her way out the door, when she heard her name called.

"Miss Swanson? Could you come back here, please? I need to speak to you a minute."

Mr. Jolly was sitting at his desk, smiling. Rosie made a smooth U-turn and headed back in through the door. She liked being called Miss Swanson. It made her feel mature.

"Have a seat," said Mr. Jolly, nicely. Then he reached way back into the top drawer and pulled out several little yellow notes. Rosie watched in silence as he smoothed out each one and stacked them on the desktop.

"I'm sorry, Rosie, but I'm afraid I'm going to have to speak to you about these again," he said. "I was really hoping that our talk last week was going to put an end to the note writing. But since then, you've written me this many more."

Rosie pushed her red glasses back up on her nose and leaned in for a closer look.

"Did you get the one I just put in a minute ago? The one about you-know-who cheating on her you-know-what?"

Mr. Jolly didn't reply. Instead, he picked up the stack of little yellow papers and began to read:

"Dear Mr. J.
Michael P. was in the girls' bathroom.
> Your friend,
> R. Swanson"

Rosie nodded solemnly and leaned in closer. "I don't think it was an *accident,* either. If you get my drift."

Mr. Jolly shifted in his seat uncomfortably.

"Note number two," he continued.

"Dear Mr. J.
At lunch, Mona Snyder chewed up her ham
sandwich and opened her mouth and showed
everybody.

> Your helper,
> R. Swanson"

This time, Rosie made a face. "I couldn't
eat my raisin cookie after that, sir."

Mr. Jolly rolled his eyes and went on.

"Dear Mr. J.
Ronald M. blew his nose in the drinking
fountain.

> Yours truly,
> R. Swanson"

"Yes, sir. Without a Kleenex," Rosie re-
called grimly. "He just held this one nostril
closed and blew out of the other one."

She paused a moment. "I think it's called a
farmer's blow."

Mr. Jolly held up his hand for Rosie to stop.
"Please, I don't need the details. To tell you
the truth, I don't really think I needed to know
any of these things at all."

20

Rosie strained her neck to see into the drawer. "But you still haven't gotten to the one about you-know-who cheating on her you-know-what."

Mr. Jolly just sighed. "Last week didn't I ask you to please stop all of this tattling? Wouldn't you rather be making friends than sneaking around like a little spy?"

Rosie shrugged. "Not really, sir. I sort of like being a sneaking little spy."

"Rosie, listen to me," the teacher pleaded. "You're in fourth grade now. You can't keep running to the teacher and tattling for the rest of your life."

Rosie bent her head back as far as it would go. "I told you before, Mr. Jolly, I'm not doing this to tattle. I'm helping you out. How can you stop all the bad stuff that's going on, unless you know about it?"

Mr. Jolly filled his cheeks with air and let it out slowly. "Look. I know that you think you're being helpful. But tattling on every little thing that goes on is not the way to get along with people. I worry about what's going to happen when the kids in here find out what you're doing."

"So what? They're not my friends. And besides, they won't find out. I'm too good at this. My grandfather was a detective. Sneaky is in my blood."

Then she paused a moment. "There's so much stuff that you don't see, Mr. J. Like how can you get Judith Topper to stop cheating if you don't even know she's doing it? I studied my spelling words, and then Judith cheats and gets the same grade. Do you think that's fair?"

Rosie was beginning to feel angry. What was so hard to understand about this?

"It's not bad, you know, telling on people," she went on. "It's for their own good. It's what you're supposed to do. It's like reporting a burglar to the police. If the police catch the guy and the judge yells at him enough, then maybe he won't do it anymore. But if he doesn't get caught, then he keeps stealing forever."

Mr. Jolly was getting a headache. "Look, Rosie. Sometimes it really *is* your duty to report certain things that you've seen. But you're carrying it too far. I only need to know the serious things. Things that are unlawful or potentially harmful."

He was silent a moment. Then the corners of his mouth turned up. "For instance, if you saw Judith Topper hiding a machine gun in her desk, you could write me a note about it."

Rosie frowned. "Come on, sir. Nobody's stupid enough to bring a machine gun to school. I mean, I've heard of kids bringing pocketknives, but—"

Quickly, Mr. Jolly interrupted. "Okay. Good. That's exactly what I'm talking about. If you hear that someone has a pocketknife, you can write me a note, and I'll certainly check it out."

Rosie raised her eyebrows. "But there's lots of other stuff besides knives that's harmful. Like last year this kid named John Paul Rice brought this big barbecue fork in his book bag and—"

Abruptly the teacher stood up. "Fine, Rosie. If you see someone carrying a big illegal fork, tell me."

Mr. Jolly put one hand on Rosie's shoulder and walked her to the door.

"How 'bout a spoon?" she asked, staring up at him. "Like one of those big metal ones that you use for stew and stuff? I bet you could really bash somebody's head in with one of those big metal—"

"No, Rosie. Not a spoon. No."

After they went over the rules one more time, Rosie Swanson finally headed for the cafeteria. Mr. Jolly took two aspirin and had a bowl of soup in the teachers' lounge. Two hours later, when his class returned from lunch and PE, he was feeling better.

Rosie strolled in through the doorway. The teacher looked over and gave her a wink. Rosie raised her red glasses and winked back.

Then, much to his surprise, she calmly walked over to his desk, pulled a small wad of napkin from her pocket, and dropped it in the top drawer.

It read:

Dear Mr. J.
During lunch, Mona S. tried to poke my eye out with a carrot.

Your spy,
R. Swanson

Five minutes later, Rosie Swanson was sitting in a yellow plastic chair outside the principal's door. Next to her, a plump kid was slumped in his seat, holding his chest.

Maxie

Rosie peered at Earl through her bangs. She hadn't expected him to be looking back at her.

He leaned in her direction. "I'm not well," he said quietly.

Rosie got up and moved.

Meanwhile, on the other side of the school in Mrs. Trout's fifth grade, Maxie Zuckerman was wrestling with a few problems of his own. . . .

The afternoon had not started out well at all. Lunch had been pleasant enough, but when he returned to the room, he found Mrs.

Trout about to pass back yesterday's math tests.

Maxie took his seat and began drumming his fingers on his desktop. Since he sat at the very last desk in his row, as usual, everyone would get to see his score before he did.

They wouldn't be nice about it, either. They *never* were.

David Underwood was the first to see it. Maxie heard him moan.

"Gee. What d'ya know. Zuckerman got another A plus." He leaned his head out into the row and looked back. "Get a life, Zuckerman," he said disgustedly.

David slapped the test paper down on the desk behind him. Melissa Waterman looked at it and frowned.

"Dork," she muttered, as she passed it to the person behind her.

Maxie could feel himself getting annoyed. As usual, their teasing was getting to him.

"Give it here, you guys!"

The test was handed back to Daniel Wieczkiewicz. Daniel W. sat at the desk right in front of Maxie's. It was just one of many misfortunes that resulted from being seated in alphabetical order.

28

As soon as Daniel W. got the paper, he spun around in his seat and grinned. There was dried milk on his mouth, left over from breakfast.

"Here you go, Mr. Brain. Another perfect paper to take home to Mumsy and Poopsy."

Maxie grabbed for his paper. He knew from experience that Daniel W. would only pull it away, but he couldn't help it.

"I mean it, Daniel. Hand it over!"

Daniel W.'s eyes danced with mischief. "Poor kid. Don't you ever wish you were normal, like the rest of us?"

Maxie glared. "Would I have to wear food on my face?"

Daniel W. crumpled the test into a ball and tossed it on the floor. It landed next to Maxie's feet.

"You niblick," muttered Maxie under his breath.

"Oh yeah?" replied Daniel, making a fist.

Maxie smirked. It was amazing how upset kids got when they didn't know what they were being called. Even when—like now—he was only calling Daniel a golf club.

He waited a few minutes before picking his test paper off the floor. If only Mrs. Trout would move his seat to the front of the room, like he'd asked her to do, stuff like this wouldn't keep happening. Alphabetical order was so unfair.

"Sorry, kiddo," the teacher had told him the last time he had begged to be moved. "No can do."

Maxie rolled his eyes. "Yes, Mrs. Trout. Yes can do. How would *you* like it if every time you made an A on a test, the whole row made jokes about you?"

Mrs. Trout put her hand on his shoulder. "Maxie, my dear, you're a smart kid. You ought to know that kids only tease you because they see how much it bothers you. If you'd laugh it off a few times, they'd stop."

"I laugh when things are funny, Mrs. Trout." He paused for effect, then went on. "They do other stuff, too. Like when you hand out supplies, they pick out the best for themselves and send the cruddy stuff back to me. Remember those new reading workbooks you passed back yesterday? Well, mine had this little booger or something on the cover."

Mrs. Trout winced. "Please, Max. Enough.

No matter where I put people, there are going to be complaints. Alphabetical order is the best I've found so far. And unless there's a good reason why you can't sit there, I'm afraid that you're stuck."

Maxie refused to give up. "Last week when you handed back our papers, someone made a hat out of my Hats of the World report."

Gently, Mrs. Trout turned Maxie around and pointed him toward the door. "See you tomorrow," she said nicely.

She nudged him toward the door and locked it behind him. He stood on his toes and tried to look through the glass, but he wasn't tall enough to see.

"I wasn't finished yet!" he called, waving his hands in front of the little window. When she didn't come back, Maxie Zuckerman threw his arms in the air in frustration and stormed home.

Now Maxie uncrumpled his math test. He wished he could show it to Mrs. Trout, but he couldn't. In addition to being the brainiest kid in the room, he was also the scrawniest. He tried to keep his size hidden by wearing baggy clothes, but no one was fooled. And scrawny kids just didn't last long on the playground if they tattled.

Just then there was a knock on the classroom door. Before anyone could answer it, Mr. Bucky, the traveling art teacher, entered the room, pulling his work cart behind him. Until this year, Mr. Bucky had always had his own art room. But because the school was overcrowded, they had turned the art room into a new third grade during the summer.

As soon as Mrs. Trout saw Mr. Bucky, she clapped her hands to get everyone's attention.

"Time for art! Time for Mr. Bucky!" she announced loudly. "Put your books away and clear your desks, please."

Stooping over, the art teacher pulled a pile of black paper from the bottom shelf of his cart.

"This morning," he began unenthusiastically, "in honor of Columbus Day, we are going to make a sailing vessel out of construction paper. We're going to use black for the bottom and white for the sails."

Daniel W. raised his hand. "What's a vessel?" he called, just to be annoying.

Vanessa Wainwright smiled. "I know! My father's a doctor. Vessels are these little tube things that carry blood around your body."

From the back of the room, Maxie let out a loud groan. He couldn't help it. Stupid comments like that drove him crazy.

"Good, Vanessa," he said right out loud. "Real good. Christopher Columbus sailed to America in a blood vessel."

Daniel W. spun around in his seat. "Are you saying he didn't, Mr. Brain? How do you know, Mr. Brain? Were you there, Mr. Brain?"

Mr. Bucky was going from row to row, counting out paper. When he got to the last row—Maxie's row—he stared down at the few sheets in his hand and frowned.

"There's not enough black paper for the boats," he announced. "One of you will have to use another color."

Once again Daniel W. spun around. "Gee, Mr. Brain. I wonder who that will be?"

As the construction paper headed down the row, Maxie stood up. He watched as it was passed back. Four pieces of black paper. One piece of pink. Pink! What kind of stupid color was that for a ship?

He was already on his way to the front of

33

the room when Daniel W. happily put the pink paper on Maxie's desk.

"I'm sorry, Mr. Bucky," Maxie said, tucking his oversized shirt into his baggy shorts. "But I'm afraid pink is out of the question."

Mr. Bucky was losing his patience. He pointed his finger toward Maxie's chair. "This is my third class in a row, and pink is all I have left. End of conversation. Go sit down."

Maxie stood there for a second, wondering what to do next. As he headed back to his seat, he noticed that Daniel W. was at the pencil sharpener. This was his chance! In a flash, he hurried down the aisle and snatched the black paper off the top of Daniel's desk.

"Hey! Hold it! Hey!" blustered Daniel W., as soon as he saw what had happened.

But Maxie had already slid into his chair and circled his arms around the captured piece of paper, guarding it with his life.

Mr. Bucky had had quite enough. Maxie looked up just in time to see the art teacher storming down his row. Quickly, he bolted from his seat and smoothed the black paper out neatly on Daniel's desk.

"Kidding. I was just kidding, Mr. Bucky, sir," he sputtered.

The teacher glared at him a moment and then retreated.

Relieved, Maxie sat down again. When the scissors were passed back, his were rusty and hard to open.

For the next fifty minutes, Mr. Bucky instructed the class on how to fold, cut, and staple construction paper into sailing vessels. For Maxie, each step of working on his pink ship got more and more humiliating. Christopher Columbus wouldn't have been caught dead on a stupid ship like this one! Not even if Queen Isabella had said, "Take it or leave it."

Across the room, Carlton Bagget made a mistake and had to start over. When Mr. Bucky gave him a pink sheet of paper, Carlton turned and walked back to his seat.

"No thanks," he muttered. "Just give me an F."

When the hour was almost up, Mr. Bucky held his ship in the air and gave his final instructions.

"Before you staple on the sails, I want each

of you to write the name of your ship across the white sail in clear black letters. You have three names to choose from. Who knows what they are?"

Once again, Vanessa Wainwright's hand rocketed into the air. "The *Niña*, the *Pinta*, and the *Santa María*," she called. "I know those because last year we did a play and I was the *Santa María* and I was the first one into shore."

Maxie was just about to groan again, when suddenly Daniel W. whipped around and snatched Maxie's ship off the top of his desk.

"Hold it! We forgot one!" he hollered as he sprang from his chair. Then he held Maxie's ship out for all to see. "What about the *Pinkie*?"

Everyone turned around to look. Maxie grabbed for the *Pinkie*, but he couldn't reach it.

Daniel W. stood up. "The *Pinkie* brought Tinker Bell to the New World," he announced with a straight face.

The classroom exploded in loud, roaring laughter. The kind that could be heard up and down the hall.

Maxie was sick of this. He'd been laughed at before. Lots of times, in fact. But nothing had ever sounded so loud and mean.

"You fuff," he growled to Daniel W. under his breath. It only meant "puff," but it would still have made Daniel mad. The trouble was, he was laughing too hard to hear.

Finally, Mrs. Trout stepped in and made the class quiet down. Still chuckling, Daniel W. tossed the *Pinkie* over his shoulder. It landed on Maxie's desktop. Right next to his squeaky scissors.

Furious and more humiliated than he could ever remember, Maxie glared down at the scissors lying next to his pink ship. Then he grinned slyly. And before he had time to think it over, he snatched them up and quickly cut a hole in Daniel W.'s army T-shirt.

"Hey!" said Daniel, feeling a tug.

He turned around just as Maxie was spreading a small piece of the camouflage material neatly on his desk.

Calmly, Maxie put down his scissors and folded his hands.

"My oh my," he said quietly. "Look what I have done."

At 1:40 P.M., Maxie Zuckerman was sitting in the principal's office. A plump kid was lying limp on the seat next to him.

Across from them, a skinny girl with glasses was staring at them through her bangs.

Not Fair,
Not Fair,
Not Fair

Earl Wilber, Rosie Swanson, and Maxie Zuckerman peeked at one another out of the corners of their eyes. Twice Maxie and Earl caught each other and quickly looked away. Rosie thought she recognized Maxie from the playground, but the pudgy one was definitely a new kid.

Huffily, Rosie took off her glasses and cleaned them on her skirt. How could Mr. Jolly have done this to her? Vegetables could be dangerous, too, you know. Last year the kid across the street got a butter bean stuck up his nose, and his grandma had to call the paramedics.

Across from Rosie, Maxie Zuckerman folded his hands on his lap and stewed.

Not fair, not fair, not fair! he thought. *If Mrs. Trout had moved me, none of this would have happened!*

"Not fair," he blurted out loud.

Earl sat up in his seat. "Huh?" he asked hopefully, thinking that Maxie had been talking to him.

When Maxie didn't answer, Earl slumped back down in his chair.

He tried to take a deep breath and relax, but he couldn't. In addition to all his other problems, now he had to go to the bathroom. He crossed his legs, but it didn't help.

Mr. Shivers' secretary came out of his office and closed the door behind her. Then she put her hands on her hips and stared at the three of them sitting there.

"Mr. Shivers has just received an important phone call, so he'll be busy for a while. I expect the three of you to behave yourselves until he can see you."

Rosie raised her hand. "But I didn't even *do* anything," she protested.

Maxie sat taller in his seat and cleared his

40

throat. "Just for the record," he said, "I watch 'People's Court,' and this is definitely not fair."

Rosie's ears perked up. Not surprisingly, "People's Court" was her favorite show. She leaned across the aisle.

"Did you see the one where that man was suing some kid for throwing a rock at his windshield?" she whispered. "Only it turned out it wasn't a rock at all. It was—"

"Shhh!" said the secretary. "I mean it."

"String cheese," mouthed Rosie, determined to finish her sentence.

They sat there for over ten minutes before the principal's door opened. Mr. Shivers came sprinting out of his office. He had a folder in his hands and seemed to be quite frazzled. He hurried over to the secretary's desk and began whispering frantic orders as he straightened his tie.

Rosie stared at his brightly colored suit and frowned. "Our pal looks like a green bean," she muttered to no one in particular.

Earl started to laugh. He tried to hold it in, but it just sort of exploded out of his mouth.

Mr. Shivers looked up disapprovingly. "Still haven't been able to put a lid on it, eh, son?" he asked, furrowing his brow.

After a few more seconds of frantic whispering, Mr. Shivers stuck the folder under one arm and headed for the double doors that led outside to the parking lot.

"Sorry, troops," he called hurriedly to Maxie, Rosie, and Earl. "Looks like you've lucked out today. Something's come up and I have to leave. I want to see each of you bright and early Monday morning, but for now, you're off the hook."

And with that, the door closed and he was gone.

For a second or two, no one said a word. The three of them just sat there. It couldn't be true. Things like this only happened in the movies. In real life, kids never got off this easy. It was a miracle!

Maxie was the first one to stand. He got up slowly, as if he still didn't quite believe it. Then suddenly he lifted his arms toward the heavens.

"Thank you, God," he said. "Trust me. You did the right thing here."

No sooner had he said it than he felt the heavy hand of Mrs. Trumbull on his shoulder. She spun him around and handed him his hall pass. "You're the Zuckerman kid, aren't you? It's Maxie, isn't it? Did you hear the part about coming back on Monday morning, Maxie?''

Maxie nodded, but he wasn't worried. Monday was three days away. Anything could happen in three days. Mrs. Trout could change her mind and decide the whole thing had been her own fault. Or maybe Mr. Shivers would be hit in the head by string cheese on the way to school Monday morning. The important thing was that, for the moment, his prayers had been answered.

After she handed out the other two passes, Mrs. Trumbull looked at them sternly and said, "Go back to class." Then she showed the three of them into the hall and shut the door.

Relief washed over them. And for the next few seconds, they just stood there, not believing their own good fortune. Then, with smiles on their faces, they turned and headed back to their rooms.

They had gone only a few steps before Maxie came to a screeching halt. Back to his room? *Oh no!* he thought. Not back there! Not back to all those snickering faces. What a rotten thing to have to do!

"Wait a second. Hold it," he declared loudly. "I can't go back. It'll be awful! As soon

43

as I walk into the room, everyone will start laughing their heads off at me. They'll love it. I'm serious. You don't know the kind of mungos I've got to face back there."

Rosie wondered what a mungo was, but she was too upset to ask. She didn't want to go back, either. She'd always set such a good example. Now they'd think she was one of *them*.

"I didn't even *do* anything!" she announced again.

Earl felt a knot forming in his stomach. Oh geez. Oh geez. What if his class was still reading out loud? What if Mrs. Mota asked him to try once more?

He crossed his legs. "I've gotta go to the bathroom," he whined. "Do you guys think I'll get in trouble for going to the bathroom?"

Maxie shrugged. "Who will even know? Your teacher thinks you're at the principal's office, and the principal thinks you're back in—"

Abruptly, he stopped. The idea of what he was about to say took him completely by surprise. His eyes opened wide in amazement.

"Class," he whispered at last. "He thinks we're back in class."

Earl's mouth fell open. He pushed it shut.

Maxie lowered his voice to a hush. "Do you know what this means?"

He didn't wait for them to answer. "It means we could . . ."

He looked into their faces.

"*Leave.*"

For a second, the three of them just stood there, letting the idea sink into their brains. Then, one by one, they turned their heads and gazed at the big double doors at the end of the hall.

Suddenly—almost violently—Rosie began shaking her head no. What was she doing? Why was she even looking at those doors? Leaving school wasn't allowed! Where was her yellow notepad? She should be reporting this! The Zuckerman kid was actually talking about ditching school!

"That's illegal," she sputtered. "No one can just leave school!"

Rosie pulled off her glasses and nervously polished them on her skirt again. But even while she was polishing, her eyes kept drifting back to those big double doors.

Next to her, Earl Wilber rocked back and forth on his heels. *Leave?* he thought. *Just walk out and not come back?* Geez, if only he could get away with it. If *only* his mother would never find out.

Now he had to go to the bathroom worse than ever. He bolted for the boys' room across the hall.

"Wait for me, okay?" he called. "Please? I'll be right back."

Maxie looked at his watch. Could he do it? Would he do it? Leaving would take guts, that was for sure. Even if it was foolproof, just walking out of school took guts.

Rosie watched him intently. "You're not really serious about doing it, are you?"

Maxie shrugged. "Why not? Why shouldn't I? I should never have been sent to the stupid office in the first place. Why should I have to go back to class and be humiliated when it was Mr. Bucky's fault? Besides . . . who's going to know? Mrs. Trumbull told my teacher that she would dismiss me from the office. And anyway, didn't you hear the announcement? There's a teachers' meeting after school, so they won't even be checking up on us."

I'll know! thought Rosie, more upset than ever. *And I'll have to tell, too. I won't want to, but I'll have to!*

Maxie checked his watch again. The seconds were ticking away. Go or stay? He had to make a decision before some teacher came along and hustled them back to class.

"I'm going!" he blurted out. "I mean it. I'm gonna do it!"

Before he could lose his nerve, he turned and took several giant steps toward the exit doors. Earl came out of the boys' room. Maxie motioned to him.

"Let's go!" he whispered, as loud as he dared. "We're leaving!"

Rosie took a step backward. "Not me. I'm not."

Earl's legs felt rubbery. He had been thinking about it the whole time he was in the bathroom. He wanted to leave. He *really* wanted to, but . . .

"My mother will kill me," he said shakily.

"Yeah, but only if she finds out," insisted Maxie. "And guess what? She won't find out, 'cause we're not going to get caught!"

Rosie moaned out loud. "You're crazy if you go through with it," she warned sternly. "You *are* gonna get caught, and you're gonna get suspended, too."

But Maxie just poked Earl in the arm and grinned. "No we're not, are we . . . what was your name again?"

"Earl. Earl Wilber."

"Are we, Earl Wilber?"

Earl smiled. It was the first time all year that a kid had called him by name.

Earl's smile was all that Maxie Zuckerman needed. Without wasting one more second, he grabbed him by the arm, and the two of them started tearing down the hall as fast as they could go.

Rosie Swanson gasped. She had to stop them!

Life on
The Inside

Maxie was racing full speed ahead. He hit the door with a mighty thud. But instead of opening, the locked door remained closed. Maxie was knocked backward. He hit Earl in the stomach with a loud *ooomph,* and the two of them fell to the floor.

They were just getting up when Mrs. Conklin, the second-grade teacher, stuck her head into the hall.

Maxie's face went white. Thinking fast, he threw his arm around Earl's shoulder and started walking with a limp.

"Dodgeball accident," he blurted. "We're going to the nurse."

"*Mummpf,*" groaned Earl, holding his stomach.

Mrs. Conklin raised her eyebrows a moment. She glanced down the hall to Rosie, who was pretending to get a drink of water.

"Keep it down," she ordered sternly.

"*Fumph,*" said Earl.

Mrs. Conklin eyed him suspiciously before going back into her room.

Maxie grabbed him by the arm again. And with Earl still bent in half, they hurried around the corner toward the next set of exit-doors.

Emily Sweete was just coming out of the girls' lavatory when the two boys rushed past. Maxie had to sidestep to keep from knocking her down.

Emily checked to make sure she was okay. She smoothed out her new red dress and adjusted her name tag. Even though her teacher, Mrs. Petrie, already knew her name, Emily still liked wearing it. When everyone knew your name, it meant you were famous.

The two boys stopped at the end of the hall and glanced back at her nervously. They

seemed in a hurry. The small one kept looking at his watch. The big one began pacing
up and down in front of the door.

Emily Sweete fluffed her hair and started
to skip. She liked performing in front of an
audience. She had learned how to skip only
two days ago, but she was already one of the
best little skippers in the world. Grammie and
Poppie had said so.

Earl watched in horror. "Oh no! She's coming! She's going to see our faces. She'll be able
to identify us!" he squealed.

Maxie gulped. He closed his eyes and
crossed his fingers.

"Please, little girl," he prayed. "Go back to
your room. Just go."

Emily kept coming. She liked the way the
stiff crinolines made her dress bounce up and
down. When she was almost there, she twirled
around in a small circle and stopped right in
front of them.

"I can skip," she announced proudly.

Earl pulled his shirt up to hide his face.

Emily looked at him and pointed. "His zipper's down."

Quickly Maxie knelt down beside her and
turned Emily Sweete toward her classroom.

"Skip back to your room now," he suggested desperately. "We'll watch you."

Emily sighed tiredly and smoothed out her dress again. "Okay. Only I have to rest a little bit first."

She leaned over and checked to make sure her lace socks were still in place. Sometimes when she skipped, they slid inside her shoes.

"Hurry up," Maxie begged again. "Earl and I are waiting."

Earl gasped. "My name's not Earl!" he hissed from underneath his shirt. "It's . . . it's Ted!"

Emily Sweete fluffed up her crinolines and took a deep breath. "Okay. Here I go. Watch, Ted."

She waited until Earl lowered his shirt to reveal his eyes. Then she started skipping. She went from side to side in a zigzag pattern. Halfway there, she turned her head and smiled.

But her audience was gone.

After slipping out the door, Maxie made a quick check of the area and took off across the parking lot. Earl was close behind. Too close. He stepped on Maxie's heel and pulled off his shoe.

"Hey! Hold it! My shoe! My shoe!" Maxie exclaimed.

But Earl kept on going. "Run in your sock!" he blustered.

Maxie turned back, grabbed the shoe, then sped forward, ducking behind the first car he came to. Earl was already there. He was lying on his back, trying to push himself under the car to hide.

Maxie grabbed him by the leg and pulled. "Hey! What are you doing? Where are you going? We've gotta keep running!"

"She saw us! She saw our faces! We've got to hide!" blubbered Earl.

Maxie felt himself tense up. This kid was turning out to be a loon. "Come on, Earl! I *mean* it! Don't act like a slub! Let's—"

Just then, the school doors flew open. They could hear footsteps! Someone was running toward them!

Earl bolted upward. He clunked his head on the car's muffler and went back down with a thud.

Now Maxie was scared, too. He tried to swallow, but his mouth was dry. Cautiously, he peeked around the tire.

54

It was the girl from the principal's office.

Rosie Swanson dove down beside him. "I shouldn't be out here!" she exclaimed, doubling up into a little ball. "I should have just let you go! Do you know how illegal this is? Do you know how much trouble you're going to be in? You'll never get away with this. I mean it. You've got to come back!"

Maxie shook his head. "No. We can't. We're almost there!"

He tugged on Earl's leg again. "Come on, Earl! We gotta go!"

Earl managed to wriggle out from under the car. His clothes were covered with splotches of grease, and he was holding his head.

"You called me a slub," he remarked indignantly.

Maxie ignored him. "We shouldn't run at the same time. It's too risky."

His eyes scanned the parking lot. "Look," he said, pointing to the school Dumpster at the end of the lot. "See that giant trash bin down there? I'll run down there and hide. Then when it's safe for you to come, I'll give you the all clear signal."

Maxie jumped up and began swinging his arm in stiff, awkward circles around the side of his body.

"This is it, Earl. Look! This is the all clear signal."

Rosie rolled her eyes. "That's not an all clear signal. That's what guys at the airport do to show the planes where to go."

Maxie was clearly annoyed. "Oh, really? Well, guess what, Madame Pompadour—right now it's an all clear signal."

Rosie glared at him. "Fine. But if a plane lands on you down there, don't come crawling to me."

Maxie turned around and looked at the Dumpster one more time. His stomach was churning like crazy. *Do it!* he told himself. *Just do it!*

He took off. His legs felt weak beneath him, like the squeezy part of an accordion. *Keep going, keep going,* he told himself. *Just one foot in front of the other. Don't look back.*

Rosie and Earl were watching. He could feel their eyes drilling into him. That's what kept him moving. For once, he was the leader. After all those years in the back of the room, at last all eyes were on him. He was number one.

For a split second, he allowed himself to smile. Maxie Zuckerman—Numero Uno.

He was almost to the Dumpster now. Just a few more yards to go—when suddenly there was a noise behind him! Maxie's heart pounded faster. He wanted to look back, but he was too afraid. Instead, he pulled in his shoulders, ducked his head, and ran faster.

The noise was gaining on him! Maxie looked out of the corner of his eye. It was the girl! She was passing him! And Earl Wilber was right on her heels!

"No!" hollered Maxie. "Go back! We're not supposed to run at the same time! You guys have to wait for the all clear signal!"

But Rosie and Earl didn't slow down until they had reached the Dumpster.

Maxie stopped and walked. What was the use? This was like having an adventure with the Stupids.

Behind the Dumpster, Earl was huffing and puffing. He glared at Rosie angrily. "You big dummy! I told you there was no one coming!"

Rosie grabbed Earl by the collar and leaned into his face. "Well, I thought I heard something, okay?" she snapped. "And watch who you're calling a dummy, bub. The name is Rosie Swanson."

She tightened her hold. "And guess what else? Your zipper's down."

Maxie threw his hands in the air. "Knock it off, you two! I mean it! We're almost there!"

Finally, Rosie released her grip and gave Earl a little shove backward.

Red-faced, he smoothed out the front of his shirt and zipped up.

"Same to you, fella," he said foolishly.

The three of them stood there staring at the school gate. Freedom was only a few yards away.

Maxie lowered his voice. "All right—now listen. When you head for the gate, just walk real calmly, okay? Just act like everything is normal. Like you're not doing anything wrong."

Rosie started shaking her head again. "Not me. I'm not going. I told you before, I just came out here to—"

But Rosie never got a chance to finish. She was interrupted by the school bell, which began clanging off the wall.

She screamed. Normally, Rosie despised girls who screamed, but this time she couldn't help it. Her nerves were shot.

"They *found* us! *They found us!* I told you they would! It's just like in that movie Escape from Alcatraz!"

Panicking, she ducked behind Earl to hide.

Earl was not honored by her choice. "Hey! Let go of my shirt!" he demanded as he tried to swat her away. "Come on. You're stretching it!"

Maxie was the first to realize what was happening. For a moment, he lost his cool again. "A fire drill! It's a stupid fire drill! We've got to hide!"

Earl's shirt was still locked in Rosie's tight grip. For some strange reason, this seemed to concern him more than the fire drill.

"Okay, that's it, missy. You're buying me a new shirt, and I mean it. Fourteen dollars. Hand it over."

Frantically, Maxie ran to the nearest car and tried to open the door. It was locked.

"Come on, you guys! Help me! We've gotta find a place to hide! What're we—"

Suddenly, he stopped talking, and his eyes opened wide. Of course! The answer to their problem was staring them right in the face!

"Quick! In there!" he exclaimed.

And with that, Maxie Zuckerman jumped up, grabbed the edge of the metal rim, and pulled himself over the side of the Dumpster.

Rosie and Earl watched in horror as Maxie disappeared into the smelly bin. The bell went on clanging, but they didn't seem to hear it.

"Come on! Hurry up!" Maxie shouted from inside.

When they didn't come, he pulled himself up to the edge of the bin and peered over the side.

Earl and Rosie were staring back at him. Earl was holding his nose.

"Give me a break!" yelled Maxie. "It's practically empty in here! You either get in or you get expelled. Which is it gonna be?"

Earl made a sick face. He knew that Maxie was right. It was just that smelly places made him woozy.

"Now!" screamed Maxie again.

Earl was shocked into action. He let go of his nose, closed his eyes, and hurled himself at the Dumpster. Maxie tried to grab on to his pants, but Earl fell back to the ground.

"I can't make it! I can't!" he cried in desperation. "I'm dead! I'm definitely dead!" After running around wildly a moment, he screeched to a halt and folded his hands on top of his chest. "Look! Look at me! This is how I'm going to look when I'm in my coffin!"

Rosie came to her senses. "Shut up and move!" she ordered, yanking him out of the way.

Making a flying leap for the top of the Dumpster, she held on with her hands and kicked her leg over the side. Then, together, she and Maxie stood on a box and pulled a flailing Earl in on top of them.

The three hit the bottom of the Dumpster with a bang. Rosie's glasses fell off. As she grabbed for them, she rolled over into a puddle of something gooey.

"Sick!" she hollered, trying to wipe whatever it was off her new yellow skirt. Now it was on her hand. "Sick, sick, sick!"

Earl was back to holding his nose again. "I tan't breeeeth in here," he said in a funny voice.

"Shhh!" ordered Maxie. "I mean it, you two! Now shut up! They're coming out! If anyone hears us, we're doomed!"

The doors to the school flew open, and kids began pouring from the building. Within minutes, the kindergarten and first grade had covered the parking lot and completely surrounded the Dumpster.

Inside the can, Maxie, Rosie, and Earl crouched in terror and prayed they wouldn't be caught. They listened. It seemed to take forever to empty the school. Why was it taking so long?

The kindergartners began to get impatient. A few started to bang the outside of the Dumpster like a drum. One of them soon discovered that kicking it made an even louder noise than banging on it.

The kicking noise echoed off the walls. Rosie held her head. If she ever made it out of here alive, she would find that little nitwit and report him to Mr. Jim, the head janitor. The janitor who hated kids.

Meanwhile, out in the parking lot, Hannah Marshall had just been caught chewing gum.

"Dispose of it immediately," ordered her teacher, pointing to the Dumpster.

Embarrassed, Hannah walked to the side of the can and spit her gum into her hand. Then she went into a ridiculous windup and sent it flying.

Earl felt something hit his arm. A bug,

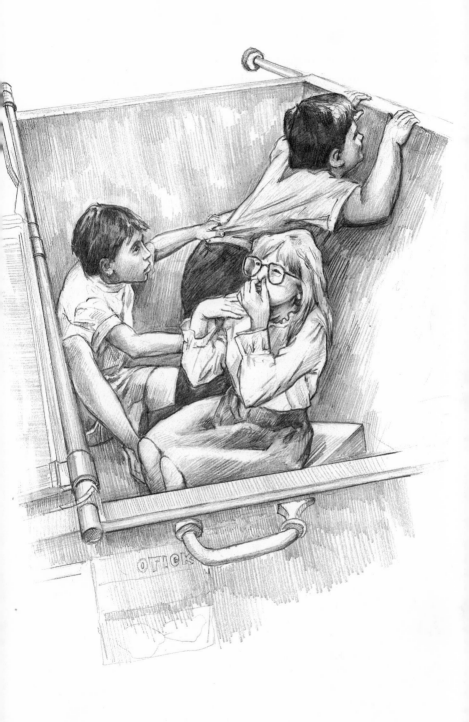

maybe? A raindrop? He pulled his arm closer and studied it carefully. His eyes opened wide in horror. He tried to flick the gum off, but it stuck to his fingernail. Trying not to gag, he scraped it on his shoe.

Maxie bit on his knuckles. His eyes darted from side to side as he waited for a teacher's head to peer over the top. Then, abruptly, he stopped looking and squeezed his eyes shut. Sometimes, if you *really* didn't want to see something, maybe it was better just not to look.

Earl felt dizzy. Afraid that his heart was about to stop, he hit himself in the chest. Dying in a giant trash can would be humiliating. Instead of going to heaven, he'd have to go to the dump and lie around with a bunch of old refrigerators.

It seemed to take forever before the bell stopped ringing and everyone began tramping back to the building. The three runaways looked at one another. Hopeful that they were out of danger, Maxie crossed his fingers and held them up for Rosie and Earl to see.

But even after the parking lot was quiet again, no one inside the Dumpster moved an inch. Fear does that to you sometimes. Even on the warmest day of the year, fear can freeze you to the bottom of a garbage bin.

It took several minutes before Maxie finally got to his feet. Slowly, he stood and raised himself to the edge of the can. Cautiously, he peeked out. The parking lot was empty. There was no one in sight. They were safe.

He turned to the others and raised his arms in victory.

Rosie rolled her eyes. "Sit down, you idiot," she grumbled.

The dismissal bell at Dooley Elementary rang at two-thirty. Twenty-eight minutes later, Maxie Zuckerman, Rosie Swanson, and Earl Wilber climbed out of the Dumpster.

They made Maxie go first.

Zuckerman
Number Ten

Earl Wilber had Pepto-Bismol for breakfast.
He put a bowl and a spoon in the sink to fool
his mother into thinking he had eaten. But
for once the thought of food made him sick.

It was nine-thirty Saturday morning. Earl
had been trying to find Maxie Zuckerman's
number in the phone book for thirty minutes.
So far he had dialed nine different numbers
and gotten nine wrong Zuckermans. Only two
of them had been polite enough to say good-
bye.

Earl looked at the next number. This one had to be the one. It just had to. He picked up the receiver.

"Earl? Are you talking to someone in the kitchen?" Mrs. Wilber called from her bathroom. "Earl? What are you doing in there?"

Earl rolled his eyes. His mother had the biggest ears in the entire world. They didn't look that big. But even when she was in the shower with the door closed, she could hear what he was doing in the kitchen.

It was spooky having a mother like that. One time she heard him sneaking a bowl of chocolate pudding all the way from Mrs. Martin's house next door. She'd called him on the phone and said. "Put it back."

Quickly, Earl hung up. "No one! Nothing!" he yelled to her, annoyed. Geez! The next thing he knew, she'd be looking around corners with a periscope!

He slid the kitchen door closed and tried again. Zuckerman number ten.

"Come on, come on," he whispered, crossing his fingers.

It rang three times before someone answered.

"Hello?"

Earl took a deep breath. "Is Maxie Zuckerman there?" he asked in a hush.

For a moment, there was only silence.

"Why? Who's calling?" came the answer at last.

Earl's heart beat faster. The voice sounded familiar.

"I need to speak to Maxie Zuckerman," he said hopefully. "Is this you?"

"Yeah, okay, fine. This is Maxie, all right. Now who's this? Mr. Whispers?"

Earl breathed a huge sigh of relief. He looked around to make sure his mother wasn't lurking. Then he cupped his hand around his mouth and whispered into the mouthpiece.

"It's me. It's Earl Wilber."

At the other end of the line, Maxie looked into the receiver and frowned.

"Earl Wilber?" he asked curiously. "What's wrong? Why are you whispering?"

Earl listened for his mother. "Wait," he said softly. "Hold on a second."

He put the phone on the table and looked down the hall. Then, just to be sure, he went into the living room and checked behind the couch and chairs. When he was certain that it was safe, he went back into the kitchen.

"Maxie? You still there?" he asked.

Maxie nodded. "I can hardly hear you. Why are you being so weird? What's wrong?"

Earl swallowed hard. A shudder went through his body as he cupped his hand around the receiver again and delivered the worst news of his life.

"Somebody saw us."

Maxie froze. For a moment or two he felt unable to breathe. He stared into the phone.

"No," he breathed in a hush. "No way."

"Yes way," insisted Earl. "I *saw* him. I saw him see us."

This time there was no response.

Earl got tired of waiting. "Well, aren't you going to say something? Don't you want to know who it was?"

Still there was no answer.

"Mr. Jim, that's who."

Now Maxie groaned. Oh, God, no! It was worse than he thought.

He took a deep breath. "Are you sure?" he asked, shaken. "Are you sure it was Mr. Jim? The janitor who hates kids? The one with the bleeding dragon tattoo on his arm?"

69

Earl nodded. Yup. That was the Mr. Jim, all right.

"He was coming around the corner with his bucket with the wheels on it and he saw me climbing out of the Dumpster. You and Rosie had already started to run. But he saw all of us. I'm positive. He folded his arms and just watched us go. You were both running in different directions, so I couldn't catch up with you."

By this time, all the color had drained out of Maxie's face.

"You're *positive* it was Mr. Jim, right? Was he wearing black high-tops? Did his bucket have a little skull painted on the side of it?"

Earl closed his eyes and gulped at the thought of who they were dealing with. "Come on, Maxie. You've got to get us out of this. You've just *got* to."

Maxie put the phone down on the kitchen table and laid his head next to his cereal bowl. He knew Earl was still there, but his body was suddenly limp, and he needed a moment to recover.

Outside, Mr. Zuckerman was mowing the lawn. Maxie could see him between the slats of the miniblinds. Just looking at his father

made him feel queasy. Mr. Zuckerman was not a reasonable man about things like this. Like, someday they would never look back on this and laugh.

On the other end of the line, Earl Wilber was going crazy.

"Pssst! Maxie! *Maxie!* Are you still there? Come on! Answer me! Oh geez, you didn't hang up, did you?"

Maxie made a face. The kid was making him crazy. He picked up the receiver. "For crying out loud, Earl. Give me a second, wouldja? Wouldja just give me a second? I've gotta think, don't I?"

"Maybe I should call that girl Rosie," offered Earl. "Maybe she can help us figure out what to do. At least we could get our stories straight. That's important, don't you think? That we all tell the same story?"

Maxie was still staring out the blinds at his dad. For some reason, his father looked bigger than he used to. Could he have grown?

Earl was getting desperate. "Geez, Maxie. *Say* something. Don't do this to me. We've got to meet somewhere. It's *important!*"

He stopped a moment to listen for his mother again.

"We could meet here, but my mother has these gigantic ears you wouldn't believe. I mean, they look sort of normal, but—"

Maxie didn't hear the rest. Mr. Zuckerman was just coming in the kitchen door.

"Dad! Hi! Hi, Dad!" Maxie blurted out.

Why was his voice so loud? Why was he repeating himself? *Act normal! Just act normal!*

Maxie took a deep breath. "Been mowin', Dad?" Quickly, he looked out the window. "Yup, you've been mowin', all right. Hot out there? Need a drink of water?"

Mr. Zuckerman eyed his son suspiciously. "You okay?"

"Me? Oh, yeah. I'm fine. I'm fine."

He held the receiver stiffly in front of him. "Just sittin' here talking to my friend Earl."

"Ted!" hissed Earl in his ear. "Call me Ted!"

Maxie's face went funny. "I mean Ted . . . Earl Ted . . . my good friend Earl Ted."

He put the receiver back to his ear. "So how're ya doing, Earl Ted?"

Mr. Zuckerman looked at his son oddly and went back outside.

Maxie winced. How could he have acted so stupid?

"I think I just had some sort of breakdown or something, Earl. I'll have to call you back."

But Earl held his ground. "No! You *can't* go yet! We've got to set up a meeting. I'll try and call Rosie. Just tell me where to meet!"

Maxie's head had started to pound. "Okay, okay. Behind my garage at noon. It's the yellow house across from the junior high. I'll see you then."

The line went dead.

Earl called "Hello, hello" into the receiver, but no one answered.

As he hung up the phone, he breathed a small sigh of relief. At least now he wasn't the only one who knew about Mr. Jim. At least now there was someone who felt just as sick as he did.

He stood up straight and took a deep breath. Quickly, he sat down again.

When his legs felt stronger, he walked to the sink and took another swig of Pepto-Bismol.

Excuses,
Excuses

Rosie left her home at eleven-forty-five. It had been an hour since she'd received the phone call from Earl, and now she was on her way to the yellow house across from the junior high.

It was unusual for Rosie to be spending the afternoon with kids her own age. She used to have a lot of playmates. But sooner or later she had been forced to tattle on them. And now she hardly got invited anywhere.

This time, though, she hadn't been invited

over to play. This time it was serious. Very serious.

All her life, her grandfather the detective had told her stories about what happens to people who break the law. One time when she visited him at the police station, she'd even met an actual criminal. He was sitting on a bench outside Granddad's office. His name was Lloyd. He had stolen a lady's purse. Lloyd said he was innocent. He said he'd only been looking for a hankie. But even though his nose was running, no one believed him.

Rosie was almost there now. Maxie's house was just across the street. She looked both ways to see if any cars were coming. That's when she saw him. A boy wearing a hooded Eskimo parka and a ski mask was heading toward her on the sidewalk.

Rosie adjusted her glasses and strained her eyes. She couldn't be sure, but for some reason she thought it might be . . .

"Earl!" she called. "Hey, Earl! Is that you? Wait up!"

Rosie didn't mind yelling at people on the street like that. Even if it wasn't Earl, she wouldn't have been embarrassed.

The boy seemed to freeze for a second. Then

he pulled the hood of the jacket even farther down over his face and darted across the street.

Rosie gave chase. "Hey, stop!" she hollered again. "I mean it, Earl! If that's you, wait for me!"

But he didn't stop running until she had chased him all the way to the end of Maxie's driveway.

Huffing and puffing, the boy pulled off the wool ski mask and threw it on the ground.

"Great!" he exclaimed. "Tell the whole world it's me, why don't you?"

Earl's face was red from running. His eyes looked tired and bloodshot.

Maxie bolted out the back of the garage. He'd been waiting in there so his father couldn't find him.

"Quiet, you guys!" he hissed, yanking them inside. "You want the whole neighborhood to hear you?"

But Earl was still scowling at Rosie. "You big stupid! You giant big stupid! You blew my cover!"

Normally, Earl was not a violent person. But he was very tense from not sleeping. And besides, his disguise had been important to him.

Sneaking the old moth-eaten fur parka out of the house without being seen had not been easy. It had to be moved in stages. First to the laundry room, then—when the coast was clear—behind the sofa, and finally out the back door, behind the bushes. It had been worth it, though. At least until Rosie the big-mouth had screamed his name all over the universe.

Rosie was not bothered one bit by Earl's yelling. It only made her more curious. She folded her arms suspiciously and glared back at him.

"I don't get this. Why the jacket and mask? Why are you being so secretive?"

Earl got suddenly quiet. He let the parka slide off his shoulders and stared at the wet spots his sweat was making on the garage floor. "Well, uh, I'm just wearing a disguise, that's all. I just sort of—you know—felt like looking like an Eskimo guy today."

He raised his eyes slightly. "Ever do that? Ever get out of bed in the morning and feel like looking like an Eskimo guy?"

Now Maxie folded his arms, too. "Why do you need a disguise, Earl?"

Earl didn't like being pressured. After a

minute, he began rocking back and forth, from his toes to his heels.

"Well, you know," he said, pulling at his collar. "I was just sort of thinking that maybe it would be better if I wasn't seen with you guys for a while, that's all."

Rosie squinted. "Why's that?"

Earl was fidgeting more and more.

"Well, I don't know. I guess I just sort of figured that maybe there was a chance that, um, you guys might get caught and, uh, well, you know—"

He stopped and forced a sick little smile.

"I might not."

Maxie frowned. "But you said that Mr. Jim saw *all* of us. He didn't just see Rosie and me."

Earl stretched out the neck of his shirt so he could breathe easier.

"Yeah, only I'm a new kid. And except for yesterday, I don't think Mr. Jim's ever seen me before. It's not like with you guys. You two have probably been around since kindergarten. I bet he can describe you in his sleep."

Maxie was angry. "That's really nice, Earl. In other words, you want the three of us to think of an excuse in case we *all* get caught. But if only me and Rosie get caught, then you'll just sort of slink away under your stupid ski mask and watch us get suspended."

Earl reached into his pocket and pulled out a pack of Rolaids.

Rosie and Maxie were disgusted. What kind of a kid was this Earl Wilber, anyway? What sort of person would just look out for himself and not care what happened to anyone else?

They were both about to start yelling, when Earl spoke up.

"I could be wrong, you know. Maybe *I'll* be the only one caught. Maybe Mr. Jim didn't see your faces. I know he saw mine, though. I'm positive of that."

Then he stopped to let them think about it.

"What will you guys do then, huh? Are you both gonna come running to the office and turn yourselves in and tell Mr. Shivers that you were with me?"

Maxie and Rosie just looked at each other. They never answered, though. They didn't have to. Everyone already knew the answer to that one. Finally, Maxie just sighed and pointed to an old car parked in the garage.

"Let's sit in there," he said. "It's more private."

The car was a '55 Chevy. Its red-and-white paint job was chipped in spots, and it was resting on four flat tires. Maxie opened the back door and motioned for Rosie and Earl to get inside. After they were settled, he looked out the garage window to make sure his father wasn't nearby. Then he got on his knees in the front seat and faced them.

"Mr. Jim's not the only problem, you know," he said somberly. "I'm a little worried about that foozle who saw us in the hall. That little fub with the name tag. Emily something."

"Sweete," blurted Earl, before thinking it over. "Emily Sweete. Daughter of Vincent. Lives on North Rosebud Lane. Phone number, 555-2 something or other."

Maxie's eyes opened wide. "How did you know that? Did you call her, Earl? Did you talk to her? What did you say?"

Earl started to fidget again. He wished he had never mentioned it.

He bent his head and lowered his voice. "Um, well . . . nothing, really. I mean, since I was already calling everybody, I called her too, you know? And then I sort of said that I was the bogeyman and that if she told anybody about the two boys in the hall, well, that I'd be paying her a little visit.''

Maxie clenched his fists in victory.

"Yes! Way to go, Earl, baby!" he exclaimed with delight. "What did she say?"

Earl turned his head and stared out the car window. It was obvious that he didn't want to answer.

"Earrrrl! What did she say?"

Earl folded his hands in his lap and stared down at them. He cleared his throat.

"She said she could skip," he mumbled quietly.

Rosie hid her face in her hands and groaned. "I *told* you this would happen. I knew you'd never get away with it. I never should have come out to save you. Now I'm in just as much trouble as you are, and I didn't even do anything!"

Maxie's arms flew into the air. "Will you please not say stuff like that? It doesn't help anything to throw that up in our faces. We're *all* caught, okay? And *you* were there, too! And I don't care if you've never done another bad thing in your entire life—you've done one now!"

Still hidden behind her hands, Rosie stuck out her tongue.

"We're going to get suspended," Maxie went on. "Unless we can think of a good excuse for why we were in the Dumpster, we're dead. Now come on! Let's put on our thinking caps and think of a way out of this!"

Earl sat there a moment. Then he quietly put on his ski mask and began to think.

Except for the sound of breathing, the car was totally silent.

"Come on," Maxie urged again, after several minutes had gone by. "Think! Think! Think!"

A moment later, Earl clapped his hands together.

"I've got an excuse," he said excitedly. "I just remembered it. My mother used it when she got caught for speeding one time, and the cop didn't even give her a ticket."

Encouraged by this breakthrough, Rosie nodded eagerly.

"Yeah? So? What was it?"

Earl looked at them hopefully through the

two round eyeholes in the wool mask. His voice grew quiet and secretive. "She told him that she had a chicken pot pie in the oven," he whispered through the mouth opening.

Rosie and Maxie stared at each other blankly.

"That's it?" Rosie asked in disbelief. "You want us to tell Mr. Shivers that we left school because we had a chicken pot pie in the oven?"

Earl felt like a fool. Why did things always sound so good in his head and so stupid out loud? Without saying another word, he took off his thinking cap and put it back on the floor.

Maxie tapped his finger on his chin in thought. "Maybe we're making this too complicated," he observed. "Maybe we should just keep it simple and say it was a mistake."

Rosie looked doubtful. "We climbed into the Dumpster by mistake?"

"Yeah. Sure. Why not?" said Maxie. "Remember when we left the office and Mrs. Trumbull said, 'Go back to class'? Well, we'll just tell Mr. Shivers we thought she said, 'Go sit in the *trash*.' "

The car was filled with silence. When Maxie

84

looked up, Rosie's eyes were staring a hole right through his head.

"Brilliant," she said dryly.

Trying to maintain some sort of dignity, Maxie turned around and, little by little, slid down on the seat and out of view.

In the corner, Earl was digging around in his pocket again. He offered Rosie a Rolaid. She took it. A second later, she made a face and spit it out on the garage floor. Now that she was a criminal, spitting didn't bother her that much.

Slyly, she raised one eyebrow. She'd been doing some thinking of her own.

"What if we offered Mr. Jim something not to tell? Like, you know . . . *money*."

"Money?" repeated Earl.

Rosie nodded eagerly. "Yeah. It's called hush money. It's when you pay people to keep their mouths shut. We could put it in an envelope and stick it in his mailbox or something."

Earl looked worried. He'd just spent his allowance on a digital thermometer and a pair of Odor-Eaters.

Maxie got up on his knees and pulled his empty pockets inside out. He scraped the lint from their seams and deposited the fuzz in Rosie's hand.

She moaned. "Great. Then we might as well face it. On Monday morning we're going to get suspended and our lives will be over and that will be that. It will go on our school records forever and ever and we won't be able to go to college or get a job and the next thing you know we'll end up in jail with a stolen purse and a runny nose."

Frantically, Earl started bouncing up and down on the seat. "No. Come on, you guys," he whined. "What if I call Mr. Jim? What if I beg him not to tell? What if I—"

Tap, tap, tap.

Earl's heart stopped. There was a man! A man was at his window!

In his panic to get out of the car, Earl lifted up on the door handle and pushed with all his might. When Mr. Zuckerman opened the door from the outside, Earl Wilber fell onto the garage floor.

Maxie hurried out of the car. Rosie followed. How long had Maxie's father been listening? How much had he heard?

"Dad! Hi! Hi, Dad!" called Maxie for the

second time that day. "These are, uh, my friends. This is Rosie, and that's, uh—"

They looked down.

"Earl."

"Ted," said Earl.

"Earl Ted," said Maxie.

Mr. Zuckerman frowned.

"It's okay we were in the car, isn't it, Dad?" Maxie continued, trying desperately to get his father's attention off Earl.

Not waiting for an answer, he turned to Rosie. "This was my dad's car when he was in high school. It almost still runs, too. All it needs is some new tires, a little body work, and a new engine. Right, Dad?"

Maxie patted the hood. "Yup. This is what you'd call a classic car. It's a collector's item. Am I correct on this, Dad? Not many of these babies around anymore, are there?"

Mr. Zuckerman was still staring at Earl. After a minute, he just shook his head in puzzlement and headed out the door.

Earl bolted up and dusted off in a fury.

"Thank you! Thank you very much!" he snapped, leaning into Maxie's face. "Thank you for telling me that your father was at the window! Thank you for letting me make a fool of myself!"

Abruptly, he reached into the car and grabbed his fur parka and ski mask from the floorboard.

Surprised at the sudden outburst, Maxie just stood there and watched.

Earl put on the heavy jacket and started for the door. He looked funny, but Maxie tried not to laugh. Next to him, Rosie was covering her mouth.

"I'm going home!" Earl declared angrily.

Maxie grabbed his arm. "No, Earl. Don't do that. Come on. Why do you have to go home?"

Rosie took her hand away from her mouth. "Maybe he has an Eskimo pie in the oven."

The two of them looked at each other and exploded into laughter.

Earl wanted to die. Why was he always being laughed at? Why were people so mean?

He tried to pull away from Maxie, but Rosie grabbed his other arm. Even though she was still laughing, she tried to make things better.

"Don't go. I'm sorry," she apologized. "Really. I was kidding."

"She *was*," insisted Maxie. "Come on, Earl.

It was just funny, that's all. Can't you see that it was just funny?"

With both of them pulling on his arms, Earl stopped struggling. Somberly, he stared down at the floor and shuffled his feet.

Then he sighed.

Maxie and Rosie each gave him a pat.

After a minute or two, the three of them got back in the car.

Only in
Books

By Sunday night, they still had not come up with a plan. Doomed and depressed at the thought of Monday morning's meeting with the principal, Maxie, Rosie, and Earl called each other on the phone and arranged to meet on the school playground at 7:30 A.M. Reluctantly, Earl agreed not to wear his ski mask.

When they arrived, it was difficult to tell which of them looked worse. Rosie and Maxie were tired and pale. Earl was wearing sunglasses.

"It's not a disguise," he said defensively.

90

"My eyes are all red and I didn't want my mother to see them."

Suddenly, he put his hand over his mouth. "I couldn't keep my breakfast down, either. I mean, it went down, but then it came right back up again. It was only half a bowl of Frosted Fiber Flakes, but it—"

Maxie covered his ears. "Okay, okay. You don't need to paint us a picture."

Weakly, Rosie sat on the swing right next to Maxie's. Her hair was stringier than usual, and her eyes looked pink and puffy through her glasses.

"It's all over. Ten years of being perfect, right down the toilet. By this afternoon, I'll probably be blowing my nose in the water fountain."

Maxie sat quiet and still. He looked at his watch: 7:46. The bell would ring in forty-four minutes. The moment of doom was closing in.

"I know Mr. Shivers knows by now," Rosie continued gloomily. "Mr. Jim probably called him as soon as he got home on Friday afternoon and blabbed the whole thing. That's the best time to report people, you know—while their faces are still fresh in your mind."

She paused a moment, then added, "At least that's what I've heard."

Maxie groaned and put his chin in his hands. "I feel like I'm at my own funeral."

Earl took his hand away from his mouth and muttered, "You are."

Just then, Mr. Jim rounded the corner of the school. He was carrying a load of paper towels into the office.

The three shuddered at the sight of him. Maxie ducked behind the slide.

He couldn't stand it anymore. The pressure had been building up inside him for too long. He jumped up.

"I don't care if he sees me or not. If I don't get this over with, I'm going to go crazy. I mean it. I am."

He took off. Boldly at first. Then more and more slowly, until finally he came to a complete stop. Sadly, he turned around and looked back. Rosie took a deep breath and joined him.

They waited for Earl. When he didn't come, they went back and got him. Then, side by side, the three of them began the long, nerve-racking trek toward the school building.

When they were almost there, Earl col-

lapsed in the grass and for a moment seemed unable to continue.

Rosie bent down and pointed her finger in his face. "If you don't get up, I'm going to hurt you."

Earl got up. The office door was only a few feet in front of them. Rosie reached out and pulled it open. They stepped inside. When Mrs. Trumbull looked up from her desk, she didn't seem surprised to see them.

"Have a seat," she said, pointing to the yellow chairs. Then she buzzed the principal in his office and went back to her typing.

Within seconds, Mr. Shivers appeared in his doorway. He was wearing a black suit. Black, as in funeral director.

He stood there a moment. And then, for no particular reason, his eyes focused on Maxie.

"Mr. Zuckerman? Would you like to step in first?"

Maxie's eyes froze in their sockets. No! Of course he didn't want to be first! Why couldn't Rosie be first? Why couldn't Earl? Why couldn't they all go in there together?

Mr. Shivers didn't wait for an answer. He put his arm on Maxie's shoulder and ushered him inside.

Maxie stood stiffly in one spot and waited as the principal walked around his huge desk.

Finally, Mr. Shivers lowered himself into his big wooden chair and folded his hands calmly in front of him.

"Okay, Mr. Zuckerman. Why don't you sit down and tell me what happened on Friday?"

Maxie stared at the floor. "You already know, though, don't you?" he replied in a hush. "You already know about *all* of it."

Mr. Shivers nodded solemnly. "Yes. But that doesn't mean that I'm not willing to hear your side of it."

Maxie didn't feel good. All morning long—no, all his life—he'd been trying to be brave, but inside it had been tearing him apart. And he wasn't sure how much longer he could hold it together. A lump formed in his throat.

"I don't have a side, Mr. Shivers," he said at last. "I couldn't think of one."

The principal leaned back in his big chair and stretched out. Then he stared and waited. Maxie didn't know for what.

Maxie wiped his nose on his sleeve. "It's just that, well, you know, these things happen sometimes, I guess. I mean, I just got real frustrated, and mad, and everything seemed

95

real unfair. And then, you know, I just did a bunch of stupid stuff without really thinking."

He paused a second, then added, "I'm only ten."

After waiting a moment to make sure he was finished, Mr. Shivers raised his eyebrows. "Anything else?"

Maxie felt desperate. "I like your tie."

Mr. Shivers couldn't help smiling. But the smile didn't change anything. "I'm going to have to call your parents, Max," he said quietly.

The words cut Maxie like a knife. It took him a moment to recover. He could feel his eyes getting wet. He stared down at the floor.

"Yeah, well . . . could you do me a favor, do you think? Could you just tell my dad that I'll meet him in the parking lot? I just don't want him storming onto the playground and carrying me off like Andy Reilly's father did last year."

As Mr. Shivers thought over what Maxie had said, his face grew puzzled. He lowered his voice.

"Andy Reilly was *suspended*, Mr. Zucker-man. Andy Reilly ditched school."

Maxie winced. "I know."

Mr. Shivers sat back. "But that's a little more serious than cutting a hole in someone's shirt, don't you think? Not that what you did wasn't serious. But I don't think your father will have to come get you."

Maxie furrowed his brow. What was going on here?

Mr. Shivers continued: "I'm going to call your parents and tell them about your little scissor party. And I expect you to buy the boy a new shirt by the end of the week. Do we understand each other?"

Maxie's mouth dropped open. Was this really happening? No, it couldn't be! Things like this only happened in books!

Mr. Shivers stood up and pointed toward the waiting room. "You can go now, Mr. Zuckerman. And on your way out, could you please send in Miss Swanson?"

Maxie nearly collapsed from the relief. That was it? Mr. Jim really hadn't squealed? He was actually free to go?

Eagerly he pulled open the office door. Rosie and Earl looked up. They were green.

He had to tell them! He had to find a way to let them know what had happened, or one of them would spill the beans for sure!

It wouldn't be easy. The principal's door

was wide open, and Maxie knew that Mr. Shivers could hear every word he said. Also, it didn't help to have nosy Mrs. Trumbull staring over her typewriter.

As they watched him, Maxie smiled broadly and wiped his forehead in relief. "Whew!" he said letting out a little gush of air. This was a hint. A hint that everything had turned out all right.

Unfortunately, Earl thought it meant that Maxie was sweaty. "Me, too," he whined, wiping the perspiration from his top lip.

Maxie rolled his eyes. He'd have to think of something else.

Quickly, he pointed to Rosie. "He wants to see you next," he said, much too loudly.

He looked at Mrs. Trumbull and smiled. When she went back to her typing, Maxie cupped his hands around his mouth.

"He . . . doesn't . . . know," he breathed, pointing over his shoulder into Mr. Shivers' office.

But Rosie wasn't paying attention. As soon as she'd heard that she was next, she had grabbed on to the counter to steady herself.

Maxie tried once more. He cleared his throat to get her to look at him.

"We're safe," he mouthed in a whisper.

Rosie squinted. She wasn't thinking clearly.

"Safe from what?" she asked right out loud.

Maxie rushed his finger to his lips. He could feel himself begin to panic. He was running out of time.

Not knowing what else to do, he took a step closer and frantically swung his arm in a big, wide circle next to his body. But Rosie only stared blankly.

Maxie tried again, only faster this time. *The all clear signal! It's all clear!* he yelled silently with his eyes.

By this time, his arm was whizzing around so fast, he thought it would come loose and fly right off his body. He was still praying for a miracle, when he heard Mr. Shivers tapping his foot behind him.

Maxie's face went pale.

"Trying to bring a plane in for a landing, Mr. Zuckerman?" he asked curiously.

For a few seconds, no one said a word.

Then the light went on in Rosie's eyes.

Thumbs Up

Earl was the last one back to the swing set. The other two held their breath as he came out of the building and trudged slowly toward them. They prayed that the eight-thirty bell wouldn't ring before they had a chance to find out what had happened. After all, it had all been up to Earl. If he didn't let their secret slip, they were home free.

Maxie crossed his fingers.

"Well?" Rosie whispered. "What happened?"

100

Earl looked confused. "He said I have to read out loud."

Maxie raised an eyebrow. "That's it? That's all he said?"

Earl shook his head no. "He also said that reading is fundamental."

Rosie was going crazy. She grabbed him by the shirt. "But nothing about the Dumpster, right, Earl? Nothing about Mr. Jim or being suspended?"

Earl pulled a Kleenex out of his shirt pocket and began dabbing his sweaty face. He knew he was acting weird, but he couldn't help it. This was like a dream. And sometimes when you believed in dreams, you found out they weren't true.

Maxie looked around to make sure no one was listening. "Are you saying what I hope you're saying?" he asked cautiously. "Are you saying that you didn't get caught, either?"

The excitement was building in Maxie's voice. "Do you mean that maybe we actually got away with this?"

Earl was still in a daze. "I don't know what I'm saying. I mean, I guess if *you* got away with it and *Rosie* got away with it and *I* got away with it . . . then I guess we got away with it. Only . . ."

He dabbed at his face again. "Only that's unbelievable. How could we get away with it? How come Mr. Jim didn't tell?"

Maxie began to grin. "Who knows? Who cares? The important thing is that he didn't."

Rosie was still worried. "*Yet*," she cautioned. "He didn't tell *yet*."

Earl nodded in agreement. "That's right. Maybe he just hasn't gotten around to it. Same for that little girl."

Maxie put his hands over his ears. "You guys are like the Gloom and Doom twins! I'm telling you it's over! Mr. Jim didn't squeal, and the little kindergarten dipsey got scared away by the bogeyman. We did it, okay? We can relax. We're safe."

Rosie and Earl looked at each other. They had to admit it was reassuring to hear the confidence in Maxie's voice.

"Wellll . . . maybe," offered Rosie hesitantly.

"Yeah . . . maybe," echoed Earl.

Maxie smiled triumphantly.

Just then, the school door opened. Mr. Jim

came outside and headed toward the play-ground with his weed trimmer.

Maxie Zuckerman was the first to hit the ground.

When the bell finally rang, Rosie Swanson left the playground in a hurry. Instead of taking her usual route to her classroom, she walked down the hall by the kindergarten classes. Sometimes the only way to get something done was to do it yourself.

Outside the classroom, several little girls were lining up to go inside. One was skip-ping up and down the hall. She was wearing a name tag.

Hurrying along beside her, Rosie tapped the little girl on the shoulder.

"Could I talk to you a minute?"

Emily Sweete stopped and smoothed out her dress. "Who are you?"

Rosie bent down. "I'm a friend of those two boys you saw in the hall on Friday. Remem-ber them?"

Emily wrinkled her nose cutely, then nod-ded. "You mean Ted and that other guy?"

"Yeah. Right. Ted and that other guy. Well,

I was just wondering . . . You didn't *tell* anybody about them, did you? I mean, about how they sort of magically vanished and everything?''

Emily put her hands on her hips. "They didn't 'magically vanished.' They went right out the door.''

Rosie winced. "Yeah, okay. But you didn't *tell* anyone about them, did you?''

Emily Sweete cupped her hands around Rosie's ear and whispered. "The cookie man called me. He said not to tell on those guys, or he'd come visit me.'' She looked puzzled. "What does he do, anyway? Does he eat all your cookies?''

Rosie took the little girl by the shoulders and nodded grimly. "Yes, Emily. Yes, he does.''

Somehow she managed to hide the smile on her face. Poor Earl. The *cookie* man.

Relaxing a little, Rosie looked around. She didn't have much time, but there was something else she was dying to know. "You didn't happen to see a boy kicking the Dumpster during the fire drill on Friday, did you, Emily? I'm pretty sure he's in kindergarten.''

The little girl's face lit up like a sunbeam.

Gleefully, she pointed to a curly-headed boy who was roughhousing at the end of the hall. "Him! Arnold Schwartz! He's in my class. He kicks everything!"

Rosie stood up and hit her fist into the palm of her hand. *Arnold Schwartz. What d'ya know. . . .*

She patted Emily on the head. Five-year-olds loved to tattle. Too bad that most of them outgrew it.

As soon as she got to class, Rosie reached into her desk and pulled out her yellow notepad. Quickly, she began to print:

Dear Mrs. Petrie,
Arnold Schwartz was kicking the Dumpster during the fire drill on Friday. I know you didn't catch him, but I still think Arnold should be punished.

Rosie stared down at the message. She frowned. It felt different than some of the other notes she had written. She didn't know why, but it did.

She reread it one more time. Then slowly she picked up her pencil.

Dear Mrs. Petrie,

Arnold Schwartz was kicking the Dumpster during the fire drill on Friday. I know you didn't catch him, but I still think Arnold should be punished. Fifth graders who are ditching school by hiding inside Dumpsters should not have to put up with all that banging. It gave me a sick headache.

Satisfied, Rosie put the notepad back into her desk. When the bell for recess rang, she slipped it into her back pocket and took it outside with her.

She didn't stop walking till she got to the very end of the parking lot. She stood there a minute, looking at the Dumpster. Then suddenly she ripped the note about Arnold Schwartz from her notepad, wadded it into a ball, and sent it sailing over the side of the can.

Rosie paused for a moment of silence. Then she tucked her notepad back into her pocket and headed toward the playground.

When Maxie walked into his classroom, Mrs. Trout wasn't there yet. Daniel W. was, though. Daniel W. had been waiting for him.

"You owe me a shirt, Zuckerman!" he bellowed as soon as Maxie stepped foot in the doorway.

Maxie put his hands over his ears and continued on to his desk. After all he'd been through, Daniel Wieczkiewicz and his shirt didn't seem that important anymore.

"I want the exact same kind, too," Daniel demanded, staying right on Maxie's heels. "I mean it, Zuckerman. The *exact* same kind of green-and-brown camouflage T-shirt as the one you ruined."

Maxie rolled his eyes. "Do you realize how embarrassing it is for a person such as myself to buy a camouflage T-shirt, Daniel?" he replied coolly.

Then he grinned. "What if I just buy a white T-shirt and let something green and brown throw up on it?"

Daniel W. was just about to grab for Maxie's throat when Mrs. Trout walked into the room. She raised her eyebrows. "Problem back there?"

Daniel spun around. "Tell him that he has to buy me a new shirt."

"I think that's already been taken care of, hasn't it, Maxie?" she asked curiously.

Maxie nodded nicely.

Before Mrs. Trout had finished taking the roll, Mr. Foote, the music teacher, gave a quick knock on the door. A second later, he wheeled his portable keyboard into the room.

Mr. Foote hummed as he lifted a big cardboard box from the top of the keyboard and began passing out instruments. Every week, the procedure was the same. As he slowly walked up and down the rows, each student would reach in the box and choose the instrument he or she wanted to play for the day. There were four choices: castanets, a triangle, a wood block with drumstick, or a tambourine.

Maxie knew what he would get, of course. It was never any surprise. Daniel W. always got the last wood block and drumstick, and Maxie got the broken triangle. The one missing the little metal piece to play it with. The one you had to play with a fork from the cafeteria.

"Gee," said Maxie dryly, when it came his turn to select.

"What d'you know, Mr. Foote, sir. I get the broken triangle again."

Mr. Foote frowned. He didn't like anyone poking fun at his instruments. "There's nothing wrong with the triangle, Mr. Zuckerman."

Then he handed Maxie the fork and headed back up front.

Daniel W. spun around and laughed. "Look at the bright side," he teased. "You can play the triangle and eat a salad at the same time."

Maxie could feel his anger start to build. He wondered how much longer he could keep his cool.

In the front of the room, Mr. Foote began passing out songbooks.

"Today, as we accompany ourselves on our instruments, we're going to finish learning 'The Marines' Hymn,' " he said happily.

There were moans and groans from all over the room, but Mr. Foote ignored them.

"Page thirty-four, please."

He stood in front of his keyboard and held his hands in the air like a conductor.

"Ready?" he asked. "Instruments up!"

Daniel turned around and pointed. "Come on, come on, Zuckerman. Get that fork up," he teased.

Hearing Daniel, a few kids turned around

and laughed. But this time, Maxie remembered what he had done in the Dumpster when he'd been afraid a teacher was going to peer over the side of the can.

He simply didn't look. He just bowed his head and turned away.

That's when his eye caught the corner of his lunch sack, which was sticking out of his desk.

Maxie got an idea. As his classmates held their instruments out in front of them and got ready to play, Maxie Zuckerman snuck his hand in his desk and opened the top of the lunch bag.

"Aaaaand begin!" sang Mr. Foote, giving the downbeat.

All over the room, kids began banging and clanging on their instruments. Mr. Foote accompanied the horrible racket on the keyboard.

From the halls of Montezu-uuu-ma
To the shores of Trip-oooooo-leeeeeeeee.

Keeping a watchful eye on the music teacher, Maxie pretended to sing along with the others. Daniel W. turned around and laughed. Maxie laughed back. Disappointed, Daniel W. turned to the front again.

Maxie waited a moment, then carefully pulled the chocolate pudding snack out of his lunch bag. He opened the top.

We-eee fight our country's baaaaa-aa-tullls
On the land as on the seeeeeeeee.

Holding his triangle out in front of him, Maxie circled the inside bars lightly with his fork. Mr. Foote looked at him and nodded his approval.

Maxie nodded back. As soon as the music teacher looked away, he reached down and took a forkful of pudding.

He smiled to himself.

"The Marines' Hymn" had three verses.

By the time they had finished singing, Maxie Zuckerman was full.

Earl Wilber's class had PE at ten-fifteen. To-day, Mrs. Garcia was making them play kick-ball.

Earl was in center field. He hated center field. It was boring and hot, and nothing ever came to him.

He sat down in the grass.

Mrs. Garcia made him get up.

Suddenly, behind him, he heard a buzzing sound. Earl gulped. It sounded like . . . oh geez! It sounded like a weed trimmer! *Mr. Jim's* weed trimmer!

In a flash, Earl pulled his sunglasses from his pocket and shoved them on his face. This was it! It was all over. Soon Mr. Jim would spot him and go running to Mr. Shivers' office with the news.

Earl shot his hand in the air. He'd tell Mrs. Garcia he had to go to the bathroom. He'd tell her he was sick. Anything!

But before the PE teacher looked his way, someone kicked the ball over the head of the second baseman, and it started to roll. Earl couldn't believe his eyes! No one had kicked a ball out there all morning!

Mr. Jim stopped the weed trimmer to watch the action.

"Get it, Earl! Get the ball!" came the shouts from the infield. "Hurry! Hurry! Run!"

Earl had no choice. Keeping his head down low, he chased the ball past the janitor. He tried to keep his face covered with his hand, but it was no use. When he hurled the ball back to second base, he knew that Mr. Jim had seen him.

Earl felt sick to his stomach. He started to perspire. Mr. Jim was looking at him now. He was staring right at his face.

Earl closed his eyes and swallowed hard. When would this ever be over? Hadn't he already been through enough?

Then, without even thinking about what he was doing, Earl suddenly turned toward Mr. Jim and pulled off his sunglasses.

"We made a mistake, that's all," he sputtered, trembling. "Haven't you ever made a mistake?"

Mr. Jim continued to stare. Then, after what seemed like a very long time, he picked up the weed trimmer and got ready to go back to work. But before he started the motor, just the smallest hint of a smile appeared on his face.

He looked up and winked.

Stunned, Earl stood there a moment, unable to move. Taking a shaky breath, he wiped his sweaty palms on his pants, and winked back.

Maxie waited at the swings after school. He didn't know if the others would show up. They hadn't planned to meet or anything. He just thought they'd come, that's all.

Rosie spotted him on her way out the gate. Earl followed.

As the two walked toward him, Rosie gave Maxie a thumbs up, Maxie grinned and gave her the all clear signal. Earl saw what they were doing. He made an "okay" sign with his finger and thumb.

Abruptly, they all started talking at once. Rosie gave them the good news about Emily Sweete and told all about finding Arnold Schwartz. Earl told them about Mr. Jim.

Maxie grinned. There was still a little pudding on his face.

They began to laugh. Earl and Rosie high-fived. Maxie and Rosie low-fived. When Earl pulled out his sunglasses, Maxie jumped on his back and wrestled him to the ground.

Rosie piled on top.

Suddenly, they felt like friends.

They looked at each other and laughed louder.

Yeah.

Maybe they were.

Maxie's
Words

dipsey (dip se)—A sinker for a fishing line.
 [p. 102]

foozle (foo zel)—Fumble. [p. 81]

fub (fob)—Cheat; trick. [p. 81]

fuff (fuf)—Puff. [p. 37]

Madame Pompadour (1721–1764). A lady friend of
 King Louis XV of France. [p. 56]

mungo (mung go)—The waste produced from hard-spun
 or felted cloth. [p. 44]

niblick (nib lik)—A golf club with a slanted iron head
 for lifting the ball out of bunkers, long grass,
 etc. [p. 29]

slub (slub)—A slightly twisted roll of cotton, wool, or
 silk. [pp. 54, 55]

Barbara Park is one of today's funniest, most popular writers for middle graders. Her novels, including *Skinnybones, The Kid in the Red Jacket*, and most recently *My Mother Got Married (and Other Disasters)*, have won just about every award given by children.

Ms. Park earned a B.S. degree in education at the University of Alabama and lives in Paradise Valley, Arizona, with her husband and two sons.

Alexander Strogart was born in the Soviet Union and received her B.F.A. degree from the Pratt Institute in New York. An illustrator of many books for both children and adults, she lives in Yonkers, New York, with her husband.

PAR

Park, Barbara

Maxie, Rosie, and
Earl--partners in
grime

$13.99

DATE			